MY GARDEN

MY GARDEN

KEVIN HENKES

Greenwillow Books

An Imprint of HarperCollinsPublishers

For Altie

My mother has a garden.

I'm her helper. I water. I weed.

And I chase away the rabbits

so that they don't eat all the lettuce.

It's hard work, and my mother's garden is very nice,

but if *I* had a garden . . .

There would be no weeds, and the flowers would keep blooming and blooming and never die.

In my garden, the flowers could change color

just by my thinking about it—

pink, blue, green, purple. Even patterns.

And if you picked a flower, another one would grow

right back in its place.

In my garden, the rabbits wouldn't eat the lettuce

because the rabbits would be chocolate

and I would eat *them*.

If I planted seashells, I'd grow seashells.

If I planted jelly beans,

I'd grow a great big jelly bean bush.

Sometimes in my garden, good, unusual things

would just pop up—buttons

and umbrellas and rusty old keys.

In my garden, there would be birds and butterflies

by the hundreds,

so that the air was humming with wings.

The tomatoes would be as big as beach balls,

and the carrots would be invisible

because I don't like carrots.

At night, the morning glories would stay open,

shining like stars,

and the strawberries would glow like lanterns.

It's night now. Only the fireflies

and the porch light are glowing.

Before bed, I take one seashell from the shelf

in my room and go to the garden.

I poke the seashell into the ground.

Who knows what might happen?

I cover it up with dirt

and pat down the dirt with my foot.

"What are you doing?" asks my mother.

"Oh, nothing," I say. "Just working in the garden."

E
HEN

Henkes, Kevin.

My garden.

DATE			